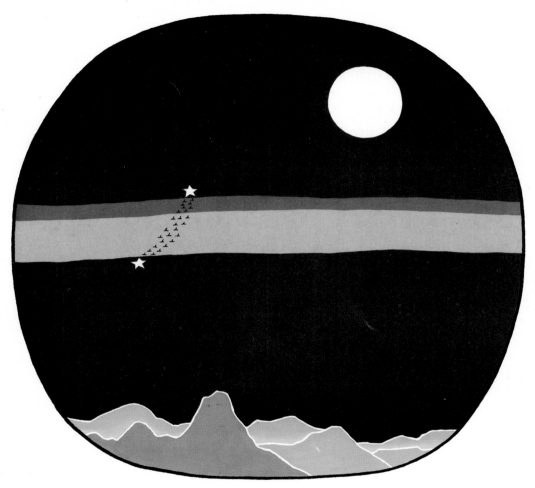

Legend of the Milky Way

RETOLD AND ILLUSTRATED BY JEANNE M. LEE

Holt, Rinehart and Winston · New York

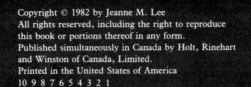

Library of Congress Cataloging in Publication Data
Lee, Jeanne M.
   Legend of the Milky Way.
   Summary: Retells the Chinese legend of the Weaver
Princess who came down from heaven to marry a mortal,
a love story represented in the stars of the Milky Way.
   [1. Folklore—China. 2. Stars—Fiction. 3. Milky
Way—Fiction] I. Title.
PZ8.1.L367Le   398.2'1'0951 [E]   81-6906
ISBN 0-03-060439-7   AACR2

To Eric and Brian

ISBN 0-03-060439-7

The Chinese tell an ancient story about the Milky Way, which they call the "Silver River."

747

Long ago in a small village in China, a peasant boy lived
in a small house by the mountainside. His only friend
was his water buffalo; together they tilled the fields
from daybreak to sundown.

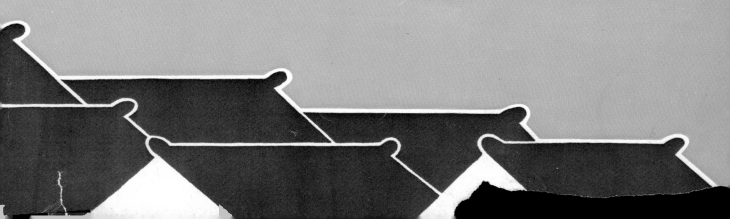

After work, the two friends relaxed on the riverbank.
While the buffalo swam, the boy played his flute.

The boy became a young man.

One evening as he sat playing his flute,
his music traveled up, up, up
to the heavenly courts.

The beautiful seventh daughter of the King of the Heavens, the weaver princess, heard it. The melody was sweet beyond words. Leaving her loom and the heavenly courts, she went down on the clouds in search of the sound.

"Who are you?" the young man asked.
"A weaver from far away,"
the princess answered.

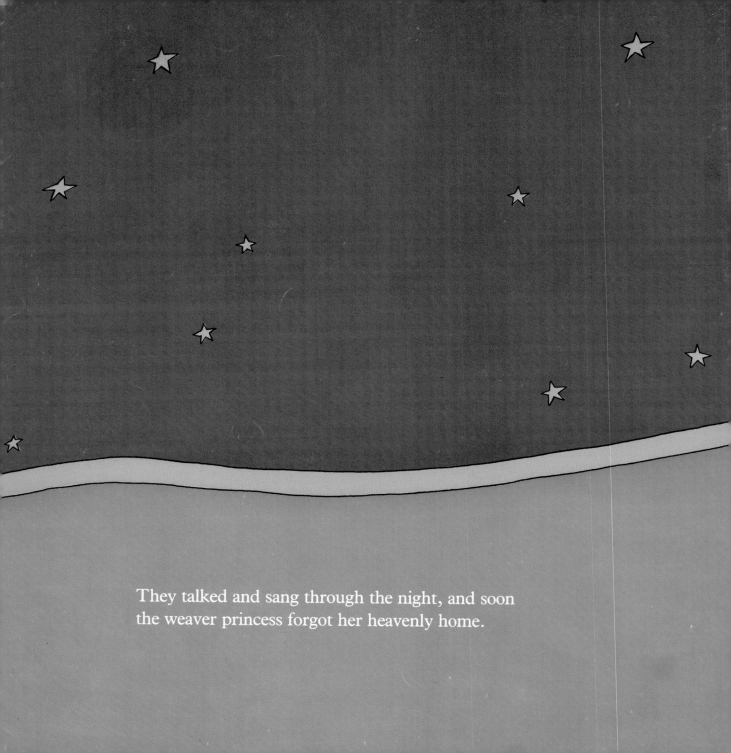

They talked and sang through the night, and soon
the weaver princess forgot her heavenly home.

She married the earthly young man
and was happy with him in his small house.

One day, the old buffalo became sick.
"Dear master," the buffalo said before he died,
"when I am gone, sew my hide into a cloak.
It will perform miracles for you."

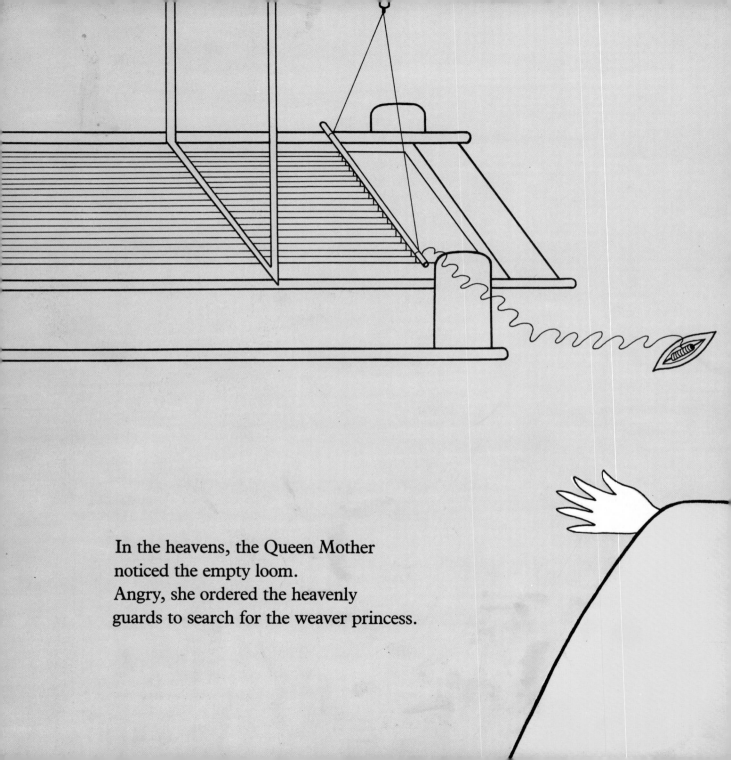

In the heavens, the Queen Mother
noticed the empty loom.
Angry, she ordered the heavenly
guards to search for the weaver princess.

They found her in her earthly home
and brought her back.

When the young man came home and found his wife
gone, he didn't know what to do. Then he remembered
the buffalo cloak and put it on. As if by magic,
he was lifted up.

The Queen Mother, who had been watching,
took a silver pin from her hair and drew
a silver river across the heavens to stop him.
He could go no further.

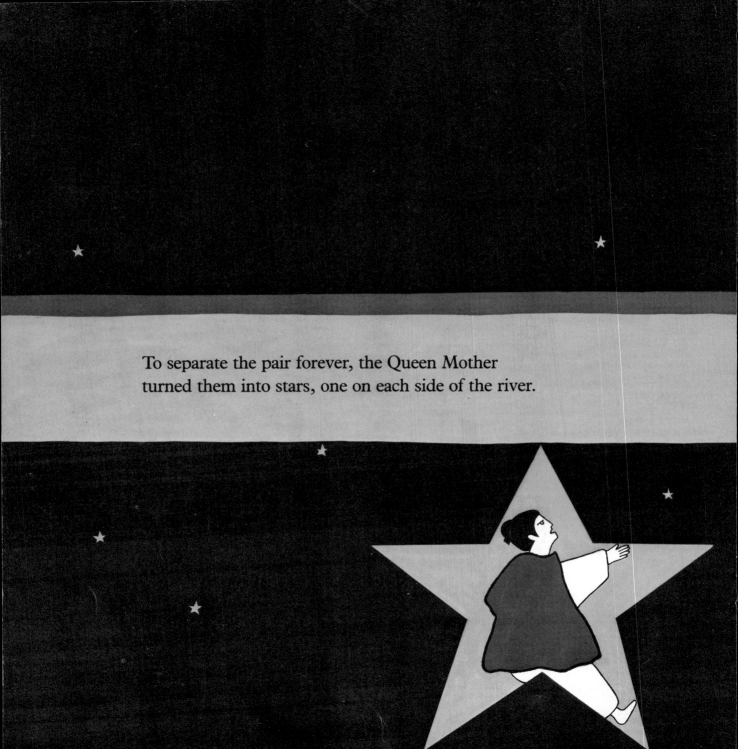

To separate the pair forever, the Queen Mother
turned them into stars, one on each side of the river.

The unhappy princess cried
from morning until night.

Her father, the King of the Heavens, took pity on her.
He persuaded the Queen to allow the couple
to visit each other once a year.

And each year, on the seventh day of the seventh month, the blackbirds of the heavens form themselves into a bridge across the Silver River, and the weaver princess crosses over to visit her earthly husband. They talk and sing for a while, then she rushes back lest the Queen Mother punish her.

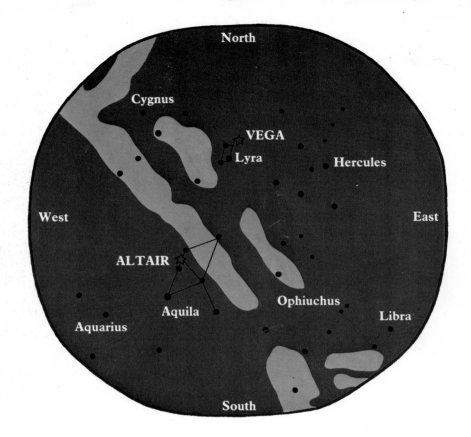

The seventh day of the seventh month of the Chinese year falls sometime in August. On that day in China, the people honor the weaver princess and her earthly husband with a feast. If it rains that night, they say the princess is crying because she must say good-bye to her husband.

Sometimes, on a clear night, you can see the bridge of birds across the "Silver River." The star that astronomers call *Vega* in the constellation *Lyra* is the weaver princess, and the star *Altair* in the constellation *Aquila* is the young man.

E
LEE   Lee, Jeanne M.
           Legend of the Milky
           Way
                        747

DATE			

WEST